MW01225288

BASEBALL

Edited by Heather Kissock

LIGHTBOX

openlightbox.com

GAME ON!

Copyright © 2016 Smartbook Media Inc. All rights reserved.

VIDEOS

WEBLINKS

PRO SOCCER KIDS

Scrimmage Games

Pro Soccer Kids BONUS Scrimmage Games SPRING 2015

SLIDESHOWS

QUIZZES

QUIZ

Baseball

Playing baseball is fun.

My friends and I love to play baseball.

READ

LIGHTBOX

Go to **www.openlightbox.com**, and enter this book's unique code.

ACCESS CODE

L B R 4 6 6 9 3

Lightbox is an all-inclusive digital solution for the teaching and learning of curriculum topics in an original, groundbreaking way. Lightbox is based on National Curriculum Standards.

OPTIMIZED FOR

✓ TABLETS
✓ WHITEBOARDS
✓ COMPUTERS
✓ AND MUCH MORE!

2

STANDARD FEATURES OF LIGHTBOX

 AUDIO High-quality narration using text-to-speech system

 VIDEOS Embedded high-definition video clips

ACTIVITIES Printable PDFs that can be emailed and graded

WEBLINKS Curated links to external, child-safe resources

SLIDESHOWS Pictorial overviews of key concepts

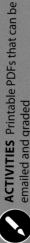 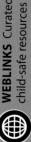 **INTERACTIVE MAPS** Interactive maps and aerial satellite imagery

 QUIZZES Ten multiple choice questions that are automatically graded and emailed for teacher assessment

  KEY WORDS Matching key concepts to their definitions

BASEBALL

In this book, you will learn

- the rules of the game
- where we play
- what we wear
- and much more!

Playing baseball is fun.

My friends and I love
to play baseball.

4

My baseball games are held at an outdoor baseball field.

The field has grass and dirt on it. There are four bases and a pitcher's mound.

The world's oldest major league baseball stadium is Fenway Park in Boston.

I change into my uniform first.
Then I lace up my cleats.
I remember to bring my baseball mitt to the game.

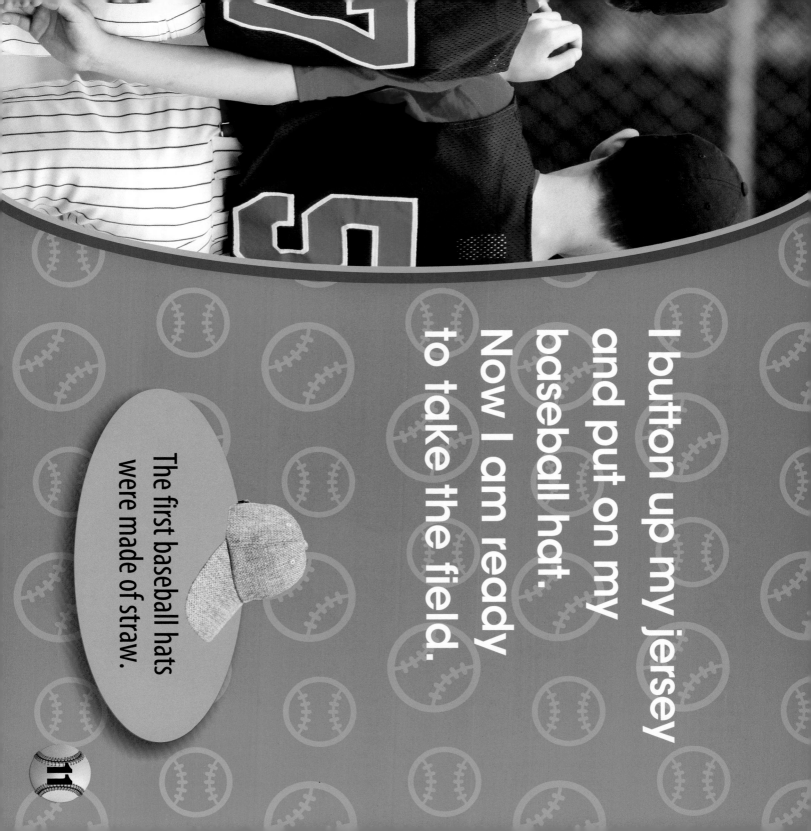

I button up my jersey
and put on my
baseball hat.
Now I am ready
to take the field.

The first baseball hats
were made of straw.

The coach gets us
ready for the game.

We play catch
to warm up.

12

The pitcher throws
the first pitch.
Game on!

We try to hit the ball
over the fence
for a home run.

A baseball
weighs about
5 ounces.

It is my turn to hit.

The ball is thrown to home plate. I hit it into the outfield with my bat.

17

The ball goes over the fence. It's a home run!

My team has scored the first run of the game.

A baseball game has nine innings.

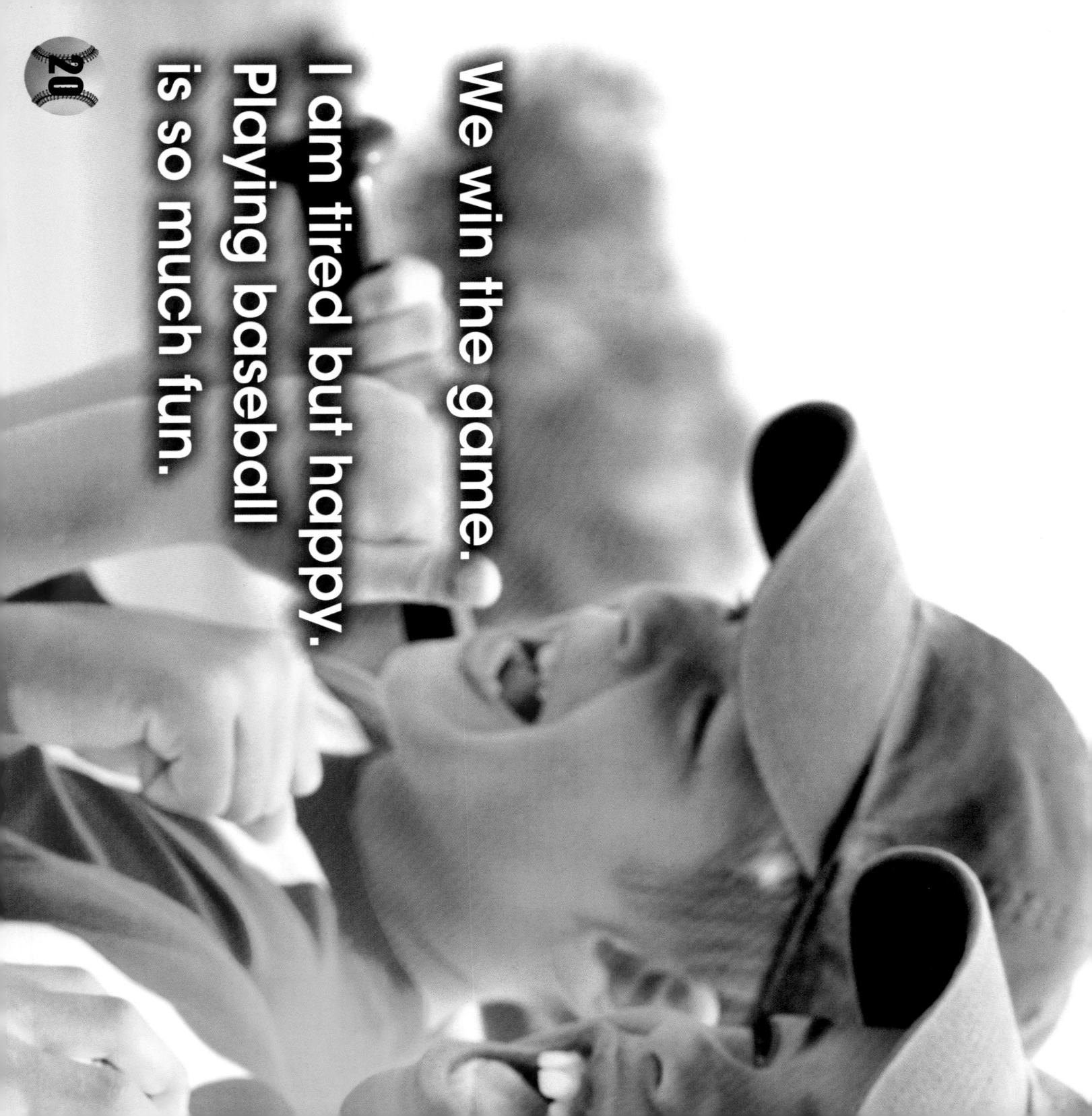

We win the game.

I am tired but happy.
Playing baseball
is so much fun.

20

BASEBALL FACTS

These pages provide detailed information that expands on the interesting facts found in the book. They are intended to be used by adults as a learning support to help young readers round out their knowledge of the game of baseball.

Pages 4–5

Baseball has been played since ancient times. Baseball may have its origins in ancient Egypt. The version played today is likely related to the English game Rounders, brought to America by English settlers. In 1869, the Cincinnati Red Stockings took the field as the first professional baseball team.

Pages 6–7

Baseball is played on a field. A baseball field has two parts, a dirt infield and a grass outfield. The infield is called the diamond because its four bases form a diamond shape. The team playing defense has nine players on the field. Six players are found in the infield, while three others play in the outfield. Infield positions include the pitcher, catcher, basemen, and shortstop.

Pages 8–9

Baseball requires protective gear. A baseball is a very hard ball encased in leather. Defensive players catch balls with leather baseball gloves that have five fingers and a pocket between the thumb and forefinger. The catcher and first baseman wear thicker, fingerless mitts that are safer for catching fast-moving balls. Players wear helmets when batting to protect their heads from fast balls.

Pages 10–11

Baseball players wear uniforms. The official little league rule book requires a baseball team to wear matching shirt, pants, stockings, and cap. Baseball cleats are recommended for traction on the field. Baseball hats in the 1840s were made of straw. In the early to middle 1900s, players began wearing hats with long, stiff brims similar to those still worn today.

The coach gets us ready for the game. We play catch to warm up.

Warmups help get players ready for the game. Warmups usually start with light activity, such as easy jogging. This kind of movement helps blood flow to the muscles so that players can run faster and swing harder. Stretching exercises are done to keep muscles loose. This helps to reduce injuries.

The pitcher throws the first pitch. **Game on!**

We try to hit the ball over the fence for a home run.

A baseball game begins with a first pitch. A youth baseball game consists of six innings, each with two halves. During each half, one team takes turns batting the ball while the other team tries to catch the ball and tag the batter out. When the batting team gets three outs, their half of the inning is over and the other team gets to bat for the inning's second half. A baseball game has no time limit.

It is my turn to bat. The ball is thrown to home plate. I hit it into the outfield with my bat!

Players score points by running the bases. A batter stands at home base and tries to hit the ball when it is pitched. If the batter hits the ball, he or she runs around the bases and tries to return to home base. Every time a batter gets to home plate, it is called a run, and is worth one point.

The ball goes over the fence. It's a home run! My team has scored the first run of the game.

A baseball game has begun.

Batters try to hit a home run. The outfield is often surrounded by a fence. If a batter hits the ball over the fence, it is called a home run. The batter, and any other players on base at the time, get to run safely around all the bases. The batting team gets one point for each player that crosses the home plate.

We win the game. I love playing baseball. How great a run!

Playing baseball is hard work, but it is also fun. Little League leaders say baseball is more about playing than it is about winning. Kids who play baseball get physical benefits such as better balance and strength. They gain emotional benefits as well, including greater self-confidence.

KEY WORDS

Research has shown that as much as 65 percent of all written material published in English is made up of 300 words. These 300 words cannot be taught using pictures or learned by sounding them out. They must be recognized by sight. This book contains 45 common sight words to help young readers improve their reading fluency and comprehension. This book also teaches young readers several important content words, such as proper nouns. These words are paired with pictures to aid in learning and improve understanding.

Published by Smartbook Media Inc.
350 5th Avenue, 59th Floor New York, NY 10118
Website: www.openlightbox.com

Copyright © 2016 Smartbook Media Inc.
All rights reserved. No part of this publication may be reproduced, stored in a retrieval system, or transmitted in any form or by any means, electronic, mechanical, photocopying, recording, or otherwise, without the prior written permission of the publisher.

Library of Congress Control Number: 2015942503

ISBN 978-1-5105-0196-6 (hardcover)
ISBN 978-1-5105-0197-3 (multi-user eBook)

Printed in the United States of America in Brainerd, Minnesota
1 2 3 4 5 6 7 8 9 0 19 18 17 16 15

062015
250515

Editor: Heather Kissock
Art Director: Terry Paulhus

Every reasonable effort has been made to trace ownership and to obtain permission to reprint copyright material. The publisher would be pleased to have any errors or omissions brought to its attention so that they may be corrected in subsequent printings.

The publisher acknowledges Getty Images, Dreamstime, and iStock as its primary image suppliers for this title.